I'm *Geronimo Stilton*'s sister.

As I'm sure you know from my brother's bestselling novels, I'm a special correspondent for *The Rodent's Gazette*, Mouse Island's most famouse newspaper. Unlike my 'fraidy mouse brother, I absolutely adore traveling, having adventures, and meeting rodents from all around the world!

The adventure I want to tell you about begins at Mouseford Academy, the school I went to when I was a young mouseling. I had such a great experience there as a student that I came back to teach a journalism class.

When I returned as a grown mouse, I met five really special students: Colette, Nicky, Pamela, Paulina, and Violet. You could hardly imagine five more different mouselings, but they became great friends right away. And they liked me so much that they decided to name their group after me: the Thea Sisters! I was so touched by that, I decided to write about their adventures. So turn the page to read a fabumouse adventure about the

THEA SISTERS!

Colette

She has a passion for clothing and style, especially anything pink. When she grows up, she wants to be a fashion editor.

Paulina

Cheerful and kind, she loves traveling and meeting rodents from all over the world. She has a magic touch when it comes to technology.

Violet

She's the bookworm of the group, and she loves learning. She enjoys classical music and dreams of becoming a famouse violinist.

THE THEA SISTERS

Nicky

She comes from Australia and is very enthusiastic about sports and nature. She loves being outside and is always ready to get up and go!

Pamela

She is a great mechanic: Give her a screwdriver and she'll fix anything! She loves pizza, which she eats every day, and she loves to cook.

Do you want to help the Thea Sisters in this new adventure? It's not hard — just follow the clues!

When you see this magnifying glass, pay attention: It means there's an important clue on the page. Each time one appears, we'll review the clues so we don't miss anything.

**ARE YOU READY?
A NEW MYSTERY AWAITS!**

Geronimo Stilton

Thea Stilton
AND THE
HOLLYWOOD HOAX

WITHDRAWN

Scholastic Inc.

ISBN 978-0-545-87242-3

Text by Thea Stilton
Original title *Colpo di scena a Hollywood*
Cover by Chiara Balleello (design) and Flavio Ferron (color) with Kristine Brideson
Illustrations by Barbara Pellizzari and Chiara Balleello (design), and Valentina Grassini (color)
Graphics by Elena Dal Maso

Special thanks to Beth Dunfey
Translated by Emily Clement
Interior design by Becky James

10 9 8 7 6 5 4 3   18 19 20

Printed in the U.S.A.   40
First printing 2016

WAKE UP, SLEEPYSNOUT!

The minute she opened her EYES that morning, Pam had a funny feeling in her fur. It just took a glance at the clock for her to realize what was wrong. She was **late**! She and the other Thea Sisters should have been ready for class half an hour ago!

The five mouselets — known as the THEA SISTERS, after their friend and teacher, Thea Stilton — were best friends. They shared rooms in the dorm at their school, Mouseford Academy.

"Coco! WAKE UP!" Pam shouted to Colette. "Let's go, sleepysnout!"

"Mmm . . . Just FIVE MORE MINUTES . . ." Colette mumbled.

"We don't have **FIVE MINUTES**! We're already late!"

Finally, Colette shook herself awake. "What time is . . . **WHAT**?! Nine?!"

She leaped to her paws and started running around *faster* than a hyperactive hamster on a treadmill. All at once Colette was

Come on, hurry up!

brushing her fur, getting dressed, and packing her **BOOK BAG**.

"How did it get so late? Why didn't Paulina and Nicky and Violet wake up?" she moaned. "They must have forgotten to set the alarm . . ."

The night before, all five friends had been up late watching a **MOVIE** — *Love in the Age of Cheese*, starring the famouse actor **Johnny Ratt**. They'd stayed up way past their usual bedtime.

Colette and Pam were almost ready when someone knocked on their door. "Mouselets! We're laaaate! **COME ONNNNN!**"

It was Paulina and Nicky, looking disheveled. Nicky's fur stuck out every which way, like a porcupine. Behind them, Violet could barely keep her eyes open. *"Yawn . . . okay, let's haul tail!"*

The five mouselets scampered downstairs and into the hallway that led to their **CLASSROOMS**.

"Hey, **LOOK**!" Pam cried, stopping suddenly. She pointed to the bulletin board, where a photo of a mouselet with a sweet smile was tacked up. "That's Jenna!"

Her friends looked at one another in confusion. "Who?" Violet asked.

"You know — Jenna, my friend from New York," Pam explained. "She lives in Los Angeles now, so I don't know what her picture is doing here . . ."

"Check it out, Pam," said Nicky. "There's a *note* from the headmaster."

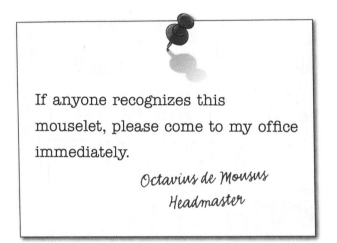

> If anyone recognizes this mouselet, please come to my office immediately.
>
> *Octavius de Mousus*
> *Headmaster*

"Let's go find him!" Pam suggested.

"But our class . . ." Violet **objected**.

Colette checked her watch. "We still have **FIVE MINUTES**. We can make it. Besides," she added, taking her friend by the paw, "if the headmaster says **'immediately'** . . ."

"We better scurry along!" Violet finished.

AN UNEXPECTED TRIP

A moment later, the mouselets were knocking timidly on the door to the headmaster's office. Inside they found a surprising scene: The usually SERIOUS headmaster was wearing kneepads over his suit pants, and he was trying to fit a YELLOW HELMET onto his snout.

Come on in!

"Oh, mouselets, come on in!" he exclaimed, putting the helmet and kneepads on his DESK. "These aren't mine, but they remind me of when I was **young**," the headmaster went on, chuckling. "Are you here for Jenna? Which one of you knows her?"

"Um, I do . . ." Pam said, stepping forward.

"Then that must be yours!" the headmaster declared, pointing to a big cardboard BOX with a pair of flaming-red in-line skates sticking out of it.

"I don't get it . . ." Pam said.

The headmaster laughed. "Oh, neither did I! This morning, the mailmouse handed me this package. At first I thought it was some BOOKS I'd ordered, but when I opened it, I realized I was mistaken. Inside I found this helmet, the kneepads, and the skates, plus the P H O T O I put up on the bulletin board. And there was a note, too."

The headmaster rummaged through the box and passed Pam a letter, which she read aloud.

Dear super-pal,

It's been too long since we've seen each other! I think about you all the time, and I miss our afternoons chattering, getting into trouble, and challenging each other to races on our in-line skates!

So I came up with a great idea: Why don't you come visit me during your next vacation? This gift is to help get you in the mood! I know you won't be able to resist it. Out here in LA there are miles of roads to skate on. I'll be waiting!!!

Love,
Your super-pal Jenna

P.S. Obviously you MUST bring all your friends. I can't wait to meet them!

By the time she'd finished reading, Pam was beaming. "Sisters, you know what I'm thinking, right?"

Colette nodded. "Better book our tickets, 'cause we're flying to California!"

"Hooray!" the **friends** cheered, hugging one another.

"AHEM . . ." the headmaster coughed. "I'm very happy for you, but right now you better fly along to your **CLASSROOMS**. School is about to start!"

The Thea Sisters scampered off to class, but their thoughts were far away, on wide beaches . . .

warmed by the California sun!

LA, HERE
WE COME!

Exactly two weeks after the package arrived, the Thea Sisters' flight was about to land. It was the **EVENING** of the first day of their fall break, and their plane was gliding gently through the pink sky toward the **LIGHTS** of the airport. The sprawling city of Los Angeles sparkled on the horizon.

Colette raised her snout from her guidebook to admire the view. She sighed **dreamily**.

Paulina grabbed the guidebook and slipped it into her backpack. "Coco, you've been reading that for hours. By now you must have it memorized!"

"I want to be prepared for this fabumouse city," said Colette. "I've already planned a complete **TOUR**!"

"Including interesting mouseums?" said Violet hopefully, leaning forward from the seat behind them.

"Scenic parks?" asked Nicky.

"Famouse PIZZERIAS?" added Pam.

Colette cleared her throat. "Um . . . actually, our first stops will be RODEO DRIVE, the street with all the high-fashion boutiques, and Hollywood Boulevard, with the Walk of Fame!"

The **friends** exchanged looks of disappointment, but Nicky took the guidebook and held it up. "Don't worry, LA is full of many amazing ATTRACTIONS — not just the ones on Colette's hit list!"

Nicky, Paulina, and Violet

It's marvemouse!

giggled, but Colette pouted.

"Oh, don't get your tail in a twist, Coco! We'll manage to do everything," Pam promised.

Pam was already looking forward to seeing Jenna. The two old pals hadn't been together in a while. She was sure that Jenna would still be the same fun, sunny mouselet she'd grown up with back in New York.

Pam was not disappointed: The moment the mouselets came through security, they heard an excited squeak echo through the arrivals terminal. "SUPER-PAM! You're heeeere!"

Jenna ran to meet her, and hugged her so tightly that Pam's bags fell from her paws.

As the friends squealed and hugged, the other THEA SISTERS had a chance to check out the blonde tornado that had swallowed up Pam.

"Um, hi . . ." Colette said at last.

"**Oops! Sorry!** You must be Pam's super-pals, the Thea Sisters!" Jenna cried enthusiastically. She **squeezed** the other four mouselets into a big group hug.

Super-Pam! You're here!

"Let's go — LA is waiting!" she said, leading her new friends to the parking lot.

The six mouselets stopped in front of a shiny pink van.

"Nice wheels," said Pam admiringly.

"Thanks. Actually, they belong to my sister, **Terri**. She uses the van for her job — she works in the movies."

"**REALLY?!**" Colette asked.

"She's a production assistant," explained Jenna. "She helps out many of the different crew members on movie sets, and she also

runs a ton of errands."

The van was stuffed with boxes, spotlights, blankets, water bottles, and scripts covered with notes.

But the THEA SISTERS didn't pay much attention to what was inside the van. They were too captivated by the sights outside its windows.

Los Angeles stretched out before them under a **SKY** that was slowly fading from orange to deep blue. The light of the sunset reflected off the **SKYSCRAPERS** and the mountains that framed the city.

"Those are the San Gabriel mountains. They separate the city of Los Angeles from the desert," explained Paulina, who'd read about the mountains in the guidebook.

"That's right! Pam told me you were brainy as a BOOKMOUSE, Paulina," cried

Jenna, taking a street lined with tall, elegant palm trees. "But tonight you all must be totally zonked from your flight. I thought we could start our **TOUR** of the city tomorrow. What do you say?"

The mouselets agreed. It had been a long **trip** from Whale Island.

"Um, there's just one thing," Pam began. "Maybe we could make a pit stop . . ."

"Oh, don't worry your sweet little snout, Pam." Jenna smiled. "I've got an excellent dinner waiting for you at home!"

"Now I know you really *are* a good friend of Pam's," Nicky said, giggling.

The van filled with laughter. Their vacation in California was off to a great start!

Los Angeles

Los Angeles is the largest metropolitan area in the United States after New York, and is located in California, on the Pacific Ocean.

The city was founded in the second half of the eighteenth century, when Spanish settlers formed a colony called *El Pueblo de Nuestra Señora la Reina de los Ángeles,* which means "The Village of Our Lady, the Queen of the Angels." The name was later shortened to Los Angeles.

LA is probably best known for being the center of the entertainment industry. It's also famous for its sunny beaches, its beautiful homes, and its great weather.

Los Angeles County is divided into more than ninety different cities and towns. The most famous ones are downtown LA, the center of business and the art scene; extravagant Beverly Hills, known for its luxurious homes and pricey shops; quirky Venice; beautiful Santa Monica; peaceful Pasadena . . . There are many to explore!

One of the most famous landmarks in Los Angeles is the Hollywood sign, which marks the heart of the movie and television industry. The word *HOLLYWOOD* is spelled out in white letters on Mount Lee in the Hollywood Hills.

A CITY WITHIN THE CITY

The next morning, Pam woke up at dawn. "Wake up, sleepysnouts!" she cried. "The early mouse gets the cheese!"

Her friends scrambled out of bed. They couldn't wait to discover the wonders of Los Angeles, the city of the stars.

"Did you know that Los Angeles County is actually made up of many cities?" Jenna asked. "There are over ninety different cities and towns, each with its own personality."

Colette's eyes looked like they were going to pop out of her snout. "How can we visit them all?"

"Have no fear, your personal tour guide is here! Today I'll be taking my new super-pals to see all my favorite spots," Jenna said.

Their day began in **HOLLYWOOD**, the heart of the film industry, with a big breakfast of FRENCH TOAST.

Then Jenna took them to the Walk of Fame, the street with celebrities' names on stars on the sidewalk.

"Absolutely fabumouse!" Colette squeaked. "Wouldn't it be incredible to have your NAME here?"

"Oh, Colette," Paulina said, "there are so many more IMPORTANT things in life, like —"

"Hey, look," Nicky interrupted. "Isn't that the star of *The Mouselor*?" she asked, pointing to a rodent surrounded by a crowd of fans.

"Where, where?" squeaked Paulina. She scurried over to ask for his AUTOGRAPH.

"I guess even practical Paulina gets STARSTRUCK sometimes," said Nicky, grinning.

Their tour continued at the CHINESE THEATER, a famous cinema that looks like a palace.

Wait for me!

Then the mouselets left Hollywood and drove along Mulholland Drive, a long street that winds through the hills.

Their next stop was the Getty Center, a cultural institute with a gorgeous garden. There they visited a mouseum full of interesting artwork. The six mice spent an hour strolling through its galleries.

"Mouselets, if I have to look at another picture of fruit, I'm going to bite into it," Pam moaned at last. "Doesn't this place have a cafeteria?"

How lovely!

Jenna laughed. "I have a better idea. Let's have a picnic outside on the grounds! I packed some sandwiches."

The Thea Sisters agreed, and

soon they were sitting on the Center's terrace, enjoying a spectacular view of the city.

"What's next?" Pam asked between bites.

Jenna grinned. "I've **planned** an afternoon of relaxation in one of my favorite spots in all of LA. But for that, we'll need these!" She pulled hats, sunscreen, and bathing suits out of her backpack.

"We're going to the beach?" Colette asked.

Jenna nodded. "Yep, to Malibu. It's got more than twenty miles of beautiful beaches!"

"Awesome! But we'll need to keep our energy up if we're going to swim. So, uh, Jenna, are you going to eat that **hot dog**?" Pam asked.

The other Thea Sisters burst out laughing. They were feeling right at home in LA!

UNEXPECTED NEWS

As soon as Jenna and the Thea Sisters got home from SIGHTSEEING, Violet sprawled out on the sofa. "I want to sleep for three whole days . . ."

"But we still need to go skating," Pam protested. She couldn't wait to try out the skates Jenna had sent her.

"Okay, okay," moaned Violet. "Let me just close my eyes for a quick ratnap . . ."

Meanwhile, Nicky began going through the PHOTOS she'd taken that day. The others crowded around her.

"You're so funny in that hat, Paulina!"

"And there you are, Coco, making friends with that puppy in the pink sweater! Remember? Coco?"

Colette didn't answer. Her eyes were

GLUED to the TV.

"Hey, what's going on? Bad news?" said Nicky.

Colette nodded. "The newscaster just announced that LANE RATLORD has **DISAPPEARED**!"

Violet's eyes popped open again.

"Lane who?" asked Pam.

"Ratlord! THE PRINCESS OF MOUSITANIA! She's disappeared into thin air!"

The friends all turned to the news broadcast. "The princess was supposed to attend a benefit party yesterday afternoon, but she never arrived. There's been no **NEWS** of her since, but the royal family has not yet officially confirmed her disappearance . . ."

"Who knows where she's **gone**? I hope nothing bad happened to her," Paulina said, worried.

"You're squeaking as if she was one of your **CLASSMATES!**" Jenna said, surprised. "I've never even heard of Mousitania."

"It's a tiny country famous for its stringed instruments. I have a **Violin** that was made there," Violet explained.

"The **PRINCESS** seems like a really nice mouselet," Colette continued.

"I'm sure they'll find her soon," Nicky said.

Just then, a **key** turned in the apartment door. "Sis, is that you?" called a mouselet a

MISSING?

Princess Lane Ratlord, heir to the throne of Mousitania

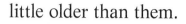

little older than them.

"Terri! At last!" Jenna cried, running to **hug** her. "Mouselets, this is my big sister."

The THEA SISTERS introduced themselves, and Colette asked Terri about her job. "It must be great to be around all those Hollywood stars every day."

"Yes, well, they aren't all so nice . . ." Terri said, grinning.

"But what an opportunity! To work on a real-life movie set . . ." cried Nicky.

"Well, some days all I do is **RUN** around like a rat with a trap on its tail. But my job can also be really exciting sometimes."

"What's it like on set?" Paulina asked.

Terri looked at the curious snouts around her. "Why don't you all come see tomorrow? I'd be happy to show you mice around the movie set!"

"How fabumouse!" cried Pam.

The Thea Sisters exchanged a look of excitement. Terri was inviting them into the heart of **HOLLYWOOD**!

"You're amazing, sis!" Jenna cheered. She turned to the Thea Sisters. "This is going to be **UNFORGETTABLE**!"

LET'S HIT THE SET!

The next day, Pam woke up early. "On your paws, sisters! Time for breakfast! And then let's hit the set!"

Violet reluctantly opened her eyes. "Mmm . . . just FIVE MORE MINUTES . . ." she groaned.

But Colette jumped right up. "Okay, so what should I wear? Something SPORTY . . . or something simple but **classy** . . . or . . ."

Nicky was already up and stretching. "VI, COCO, COME ON, IT'S BREAKFAST TIME! If you don't move your tails, Pam will leave you nothing but CHEESE RINDS!"

Five more minutes!

The mouselets burst out laughing. A few minutes later, they were dressed, and they scurried downstairs to join Jenna and Terri for a big breakfast of PANCAKES drizzled with melted cheese and honey.

When the last **pancake** had disappeared, Terri asked, "Mouselets, are you ready?"

The thought of visiting a Hollywood FILM set made the mouselets explode into cheers. "YESSSSSS!" They scrambled into their friend's van, which started with a rumble and sped onto the FREEWAY.

Half an hour later, Terri parked the VAN next to an enormouse building. "Here we are!" she said. "Hop out and take one." She pawed each mouselet a pass with her NAME on it. "You'll need these to get in."

Colette, Nicky, Pam, Paulina, Violet, and Jenna FOLLOWED Terri inside a huge

warehouse. Before them lay an incredible scene.

A **FEW STEPS** away was a street lined with storefronts. There were lots of rodents scurrying around, moving **FURNITURE**, aiming LiGHTS, and arranging props.

"B-but . . . what are we doing on another street?" asked Pam, looking around in confusion.

Terri laughed. "This isn't another street — **THIS IS THE SET!**" She took her friend by the paw and led her to the edge of a building.

"Holey cheese!" cried Pam. "What happened to the back of this building?"

"There is no back," Violet explained, joining her **friend**. "They're just pretend locations for the movie."

Pam was about to reply when a sharp squeak rose above the noise on set.

"Terrrrriiiiiiiii! Where have you been? I've been looking for you all morning!"

"Leslie! I just got here," said Terri. *Let me introduce you —*"

"Yes, yes, it's great that you have new assistants, but come with me now; we've got to set up for the next scene. Everything's a total cat-astrophe! The clothes are all wrong, the lights aren't bright enough, no one knows what time Johnny Ratt will get here, and most important, no one's brought me my COFFEE!"

"That's Leslie Mousie, the director," Terri murmured. "I have to go now. Enjoy the shoot!" And she scurried after the director.

"Moldy Brie on a baguette, did I hear that

right? **Johnny Ratt** is going to be here?!" Colette asked.

"**THAT'S RIGHT**," Jenna replied. "Terri told me he's agreed to do a small part in the **MOVIE**, and today they have to shoot his scene."

"If he ever gets here," Violet said.

"*Let's hope he makes it!*" Colette replied. "I want to ask him for an AUTOGRAPH."

"You're not the only one," said Jenna, grinning. Then she pointed to the set. "Okay, mouselets, let's get our tails in gear.

IT'S TIME TO START THE SHOOT!"

LiTTLE PROBLEMS AND BiG DISCOVERIES

The set was crowded with makeup artists, costume assistants, and tech crew. Suddenly, as the mouselets watched, the soundstage emptied out. A moment later, the director shouted, "**And . . . action!**"

A young mouse raised his clapperboard and cried, *"The Powerpaw Mouselets, scene three, take one!"*

The CLAPPERBOARD is a small board (chalkboard, whiteboard, or digital board) with information about each scene. When the top part is lifted and released, it makes its trademark clapping sound.

Then he let go of the CLAPPER, and it smacked the wooden board below it.

"The Powerpaw Mouselets . . ." Paulina murmured. "Jenna, do you know what kind of movie this is?"

"It's an **ACTION** movie!" her friend explained. "The Powerpaw Mouselets are a trio of rodents with special POWERS who save their city from villains."

Just then, three mouselets in jumpsuits burst onto the scene *CHASING* two shady-looking villains.

Leslie Mousie interrupted, SHOUTING, "Awful! Horrible! Terrible! Where is the action? Where is the tension? Where is the drama?! Take it from the top!"

She shrieked so loudly that Pam had to cover her ears. She took a STEP backward, tripping on a cable and stumbling into a cameramouse, who slipped and **bumped** into a lighting technician, who leaned against a spotlight.

CRASH!

The spotlight fell and broke into a thousand pieces . . . just inches from Leslie Mousie.

"**Rats**, what a mess!" Pam moaned.

"Who are these intruders?!" the director screamed, pointing to the THEA SiSTERS.

Terri rushed over. "They are my guests! I *introduced* them a few minutes ago —"

But Leslie Mousie didn't let her finish. "I don't care who they are, just **GET THEM OUT OF HERE**! This film is already a complete cat-astrophe without some **KLUTZ** getting her clumsy paws all over it!"

"How dare she call Pam a clumsy klutz?!" Colette fumed, her fur turning **pinker** than a cat's nose.

"Relax, Coco," Paulina whispered. "I think

Watch ouuuut!

Aaahh!

the director is just a little **anxious** about Johnny Ratt coming today . . ."

Just then, a friendly-looking **ratlet** approached. "Hey, Terri, did you bring some **friends**?"

Terri **nodded**. "Mouselets, this is Matthew, the assistant director — and one of the few rodents here who knows how to make Leslie happy!"

Matthew **laughed**. "Oh, I'm used to working with all kinds of rodents! So, is this the first time you've been to a film shoot?"

Violet nodded. "It's a new and **FASCINATING** world for us."

"Well, there's much more to see," said Matthew. "Why don't you come with me? I'll show you the green screen, one of the wonders of the **movie** world."

Matthew led them into the wing where the

next scene was being shot. The three star actors were standing in front of a large GREEN screen that covered the wall and the floor.

"But . . . where's the scenery?" asked Nicky, confused.

"Oh, we'll add the background details later with **computer** effects," Terri explained to her friends. "The screen is a neutral background that we can fill with any kind of scenery. We use this technique for scenes when the Powerpaw Mouselets run across rooftops, or fly around."

She pointed to a monitor that showed the computerized background. It really looked like the Powerpaw Mouselets were running across a rooftop!

The Thea Sisters' jaws dropped.

"That's awesome!" Nicky cried.

THE WHIMS OF
A STAR

Over the next two hours, each mouselet **discovered** a different aspect of filmmaking. Violet made friends with a **sound** technician, Colette got fashion advice from the **COSTUME** manager, Paulina learned about editing, Nicky interviewed the locations scout, and Pam just **snooped** around everywhere.

As the Thea Sisters admired the set of the **POOL** where the Powerpaw Mouselets would be staging their next rescue, Terri scurried over.

"He's landed! **He's here!**"

Leslie Mousie grew paler than a slice of fresh mozzarella. "But . . . **he's early**! We still have three scenes to film before his!"

The THEA SISTERS grinned. Soon they'd see the famous Johnny Ratt, in the fur!

Chaos broke out across the set. The crew adjusted the lights and microphones, and the

Move iiiiit!

assistants **scampered** here and there. Even the Powerpaw Mouselets, who'd seemed **tougher** than a pack of tomcats, were all jitters.

A few minutes later, a group of rodents dressed all in **BLACK** swept onto the set.

"Who are they?" asked Paulina, **confused**.

"Bodyguards," Terri whispered. "For . . ."

"**JOHNNY RATT!**" squealed Colette. The ring of rodents had opened to reveal a dashingly handsome mouse. He was dressed *elegantly* and wore dark sunglasses.

Leslie Mousie ran to greet him. "Mr. Ratt, **WeLCome** . . ."

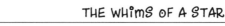

The famouse actor stuck his snout in the air. "Please don't tell me I have to act in this **rat-trap**! Haven't you read my contract? I've been nominated for seven MOUSCARS, you know!"

"He doesn't seem very **nice**," Violet murmured.

The actor had **Approached** the movie's three stars. "I hope you are all professionals. I hate doing more than one take!"

The Powerpaw Mouselets just rolled their eyes.

"Jeanette! Fresh **grapes**!" Ratt cried.

A kind-looking rodent scurried to his side and pawed him a **bunch** of grapes.

"Are you joking? These grapes are **green**!

I only eat **RED** grapes! It's in my contract!"

"B-but I c-could only find these . . ."
stuttered his assistant.

"Hmpf! This day is off to a terrible start!"
Ratt **grumbled**. Then he stomped away.

Terri scampered over to Jeanette, whose
ears were drooping.

"Don't worry — I'm sure someone can take you to the SUPERMARKET," she whispered.

Meanwhile, Johnny Ratt and the first Powerpaw Mouselet began **rehearsing** his scene, which took place after the Powerpaw Mouselets had saved a train full of passengers from the EVIL Mr. K.

The **set** looked like a train car, with extras playing passengers still **upset** by the danger they'd escaped. In the scene, Johnny Ratt was the only one to notice the *fleeing* Powerpaw Mouselet. He stopped her and tried to learn her secret identity.

"*The Powerpaw Mouselets*, scene six, take one!" shouted the rodent with the **CLAPPERBOARD**.

"Wait!" shouted Johnny Ratt, grabbing the fleeing mouselet by the paw. "Tell me who you are!"

"I am —"

"Iris!" shouted Ratt.

Terri turned WHITER than a Brie rind. "That's not the right line . . ."

"Esmeralda," corrected the Powerpaw Mouselet.

"WHO CARES about Esmeralda! Someone here is wearing iris perfume, and I am allergic! How could you not know that! It'll take me a half hour to recover!" the actor complained.

The director put her snout in her paws in despair.

The Thea Sisters stifled their giggles.

"Something tells me this scene is going to take a long, LOOOOOONG time to shoot," Colette observed, shaking her snout.

A STROLL ALONG RODEO DRIVE

After Johnny Ratt had finally **filmed** all his scenes and driven the cast and crew to distraction, he announced that his JET was waiting for him. He had to return to his penthouse in New York so he could do a series of interviews before Mouscar NIGHT.

"We're free at last!" Jenna sighed with relief.

Colette nodded. "In his **MOVIES**, Johnny Ratt is always so kind and romantic . . . but in real life he's so moody and demanding!"

"Never trust appearances," Violet said wisely.

"Mouselets, I've got news," cried Terri,

scurrying over. "Leslie has decided to film a few scenes out in the city. We're heading **downtown**."

The whole crew was going to Rodeo Drive, the street in Beverly Hills that is famouse for its FANCY SHOPS.

Colette couldn't contain her squeal of enthusiasm. This was the moment she'd been dreaming of since she first set paw in Los Angeles!

The minute they arrived on Rodeo Drive,

Hooray!

Colette was entranced. She couldn't tear her EYES away from the shop windows. The street was lined with elegant jewelers and clothing boutiques. For a fashion mouse like Colette, it was a little slice of heaven!

Suddenly, a **mouselet** wearing a cap and big sunglasses scampered around the corner of a building, drawing Colette's attention.

"Coco! What are you doing over there, daydreaming?" called Nicky.

"Sorry! I'm coming. It's just I thought I recognized that mouselet . . ." said Colette, pointing to the young mouse, who was scurrying away.

"It must be a famouse actor. This place is crawling with celebrities!" said Pam. "But now let's shake a tail, the crew is ready to start shooting."

The Powerpaw Mouselets had to shoot a scene in which they climbed out of a store window. But the director was grouchier than a groundhog after the long morning with Johnny Ratt, and she kept interrupting, forcing the actors to PERFORM the same scene over and over.

"Snout up, Julia! Lindsay, stop pouting! Cate, I can't even see you, get in the frame . . . No, now you're blocking Julia, move your tail! Over more! Now you're too far over . . ."

The actors looked worn out. Even the Thea Sisters were starting to feel tired after all the day's EXCITEMENT.

"Cheese niblets, don't you movie mice ever take a break?" Violet asked Terri, trying to hold back a yawn.

"And don't you ever stop for a snack?" Pam moaned, grabbing her STOMACH, which

was starting to gurgle.

Terri laughed. "Didn't I warn you this work wasn't always FUN? Why don't you go back home with Jenna and wait for me there? You can take my van — I'll grab a TAXI."

The mouselets exchanged a look. They were ready to accept her invitation. All except Colette, who was too busy GAZING into the store windows.

But at last her eyelids started to droop, and exhaustion got the better of her. She and the other mouselets scrambled into the van and headed back to the house.

A LITTLE REST AND RELAXATION

Back at the house, the Thea Sisters could finally relax. They'd had no idea that a day on SET would be so draining!

Pam DASHED into the kitchen and began whipping up a snack, while the others chatted about the day's events.

"The shoot was so exciting!" Paulina declared with a sigh.

"The cast was so good," Nicky said. "Julia was my favorite. She's such a natural!"

"I liked Lindsay — she's so carefree," Colette said.

"And did you notice how nice Matthew is?" Violet commented. "Poor guy, the director doesn't treat him too well!"

"Yeah, Matthew is a really sweet rodent," said Jenna. "He and my sister work together very closely."

"I smell romance!" Colette joked. She loved matchmousing. But Violet looked a little down in the snout at the thought of Terri and Matthew together.

"Oh no, there's nothing like that going on," said Jenna. "They're just good friends."

Violet perked up right away — and Colette noticed. "What's up, Vi? Are you crushing on Matthew?" she asked slyly.

"I don't know what you're squeaking about, Coco. He's just . . . nice, that's all!" Violet protested, blushing.

Before Colette could reply, Pam scurried into the room. "Sisters, DINNER is served!" she declared, unveiling a VEGETABLE pizza.

"Let's save some for Terri," Violet said.

"What time will she be **home**?" asked Nicky. "We've been here for at least an hour."

"Oh, she usually finishes work late," Jenna reassured them with a *smile*.

Two hours later, though, there was still no trace of Terri, so Jenna tried giving her a call. "It's so strange. Her phone keeps *ringing* and then goes to voicemail," she said, looking worried.

Dinner is served!

"Could she have forgotten her phone

somewhere?" asked Nicky.

Jenna **shook** her snout. "Leslie Mousie calls her constantly, so she always keeps her phone close by."

After another hour, Jenna was really starting to worry.

"Why don't you try calling Matthew?" suggested Violet. "Maybe they're all stuck at the studio, and Terri can't **PiCK UP** for some reason."

"Good idea," said Jenna, dialing the assistant director. But his cell phone was off.

The **THEA SiSTERS** noticed how upset Jenna was, and they tried to cheer her up. But a half hour later, when there was still no word from Terri, the mouselets decided it was time to **TRACK HER DOWN**.

Looking for Terri

As the pink van sped back to the studio, no one squeaked a word. The Thea Sisters could tell how worried Jenna was about her sister, and they were all concerned.

"My sister and I do everything together, except when she's working and I'm studying," Jenna said for the hundredth time. "And we never forget to **TELL** each other where we're going!"

When they arrived at the studio, it was deserted. To get in, they had to show their PASSES to the guard, who asked why they were there so late at night. When they explained, the GUARD shook his snout. "There's no one here. It's been hours since everyone left."

Jenna's fur turned redder than a cheese rind. Colette quickly **TOOK CHARGE** of the situation. "Can you let us in to check? We'll be quick!"

The guard agreed, and the six mouselets

Please let us in!

scurried inside. Without the hustle and hubbub of the actors, assistants, and stage crew, the studio felt strange and a little bit creepy. The mouselets started dashing from set to set, **calling** out for Terri.

Jenna's whiskers were quivering with worry, so Violet took her 🐾🐾🐾. "Let's think. What jobs does Terri do every day? What's the last thing she usually does?"

"I . . . I think she checks to make sure everything's back where it belongs. And sometimes she gives Matthew a paw in the **editing** room . . ."

"Do you know where that is?" asked Nicky.

Jenna nodded. She led her friends to a small room full of **MONITORS** and keyboards.

"Hey, that's Terri's!" she cried, pointing to a **P H O N E** lying next to a computer.

"But **WHY** would she leave it here? Something must have happened!"

While Colette squeaked quietly to Jenna, the others started to look around carefully. Paulina found a torn **PIECE OF PAPER** on the ground. It was a drawing in the shape of an eye. It didn't seem like a **CLUE**, but no one found anything else in the room.

Suddenly, Nicky heard a muffled **noise** coming from next door. It sounded as if someone was pounding on the wall.

"**Come with me**," she told her friends. She pushed aside boxes full of old scripts that were blocking the corner of the room where the sound was coming from. As soon as they moved the boxes, the mouselets discovered a small door.

"Hey! Is someone there?" said a weak squeak on the other side of the wall.

"Terri! Is that you?" called Jenna. She turned the key sticking out of the keyhole.

Through the door was a small, DARK

Are you okay?

room filled with BOXES. Terri practically fell into her sister's open paws.

"Terri, we've been looking everywhere for you! **Are you okay?!**" Jenna cried.

"I am now that you're here . . . but I had a real scare!" Terri said, bowing her snout. "Thank goodmouse you came looking for me."

Meanwhile, the security guard had joined the mouselets, and his EYES widened in surprise when he saw Terri.

"Are you okay? How did you get locked up in the storage room?!" he asked.

Terri shook her snout. "I . . .

I have no idea!"

SABOTAGE
ON SET!

The mouselets gathered around Terri.

"Can you tell us exactly what happened?" Colette asked.

Terri nodded. "Well, once we were done shooting for the day, Matthew was in a hurry to get home. So he asked me to take the film into the editing room. But as soon as I came in, I heard a strange noise coming from the **STORAGE ROOM** next door . . ."

"The one where we found you?" asked Violet.

"Yes. It sounded like something had **fallen**, so I went in to check on it," Terri said. "But before I even had a chance to look around, the door slammed shut behind me! Maybe it was just a draft. Then the lock must have been stuck, because I couldn't open the door and get out."

Colette shook her head. "It wasn't an accident. It was honest-to-goodmouse sabotage!"

The guard's eyes narrowed. "What do you mean?"

"Someone locked the door, and then stacked BOXES up in front of it," Nicky explained.

"And look what I found!" cried Paulina, who'd been searching the storage room. "In that corner there was a small ROCK. Isn't that strange?"

"Someone must have gone into the room, used the rock to create the noise that lured you in, then locked the door behind you," Colette guessed. "At this POINT, the question is . . ."

"Who?" concluded Violet.

Terri looked at her friends. "I have no idea!"

"Did you notice anything suspicious?" Colette asked the guard.

The rodent shook his snout, **confused**. "No, but I come on watch for the night shift at nine. By then, the studio is deserted."

"This must have all happened *before* then," Nicky said.

"But who would want to lock up Terri?" Jenna asked in **disbelief**.

Where is it?!?

Colette reflected a moment. "Someone could have wanted to be in the EDITING ROOM all alone . . . maybe to look for something . . ."

Suddenly, Terri turned very pale.

"It's . . . it's n-not here!" she sputtered, sifting through the papers on the table.

"What are you looking for?" asked Jenna.

It's a cat-astrophe!

"The FILM!" cried Terri. "The film that we shot today has disappeared!"

"Keep calm and scurry on," said Colette, putting a paw around her friend. "Maybe you put it down somewhere else."

Terri shook her snout. "No, I'm sure I left it there. That's what the rodent

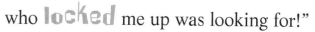

who locked me up was looking for!"

Terri collapsed into a chair. "This is a cat-astrophe! A real cat-astrophe, not the fake kind Leslie's always complaining about! It's the only copy of the film we have! Who's going to tell Leslie?"

"Oh, Terri, this isn't your fault," Paulina said. "Leslie and the crew can always shoot the scenes again, right?"

Terri SIGHED. "Maybe if it were a different day. But today we filmed the scenes with Johnny Ratt. It was so hard to find a day when he was available. Now he's gone back to New York, and it'll be impossible to get him on set again in time to finish shooting the movie!"

For a moment, it was so quiet, you could hear a cheese slice drop. The situation seemed HOPELESS, and none of the mice knew what to say.

"Well, mouselets, what do you say we head home? We can tackle this tomorrow, after a good night's sleep. That should clear our heads," Pam suggested.

"Good idea," said Colette. "Terri needs to rest after everything she's been through. And tomorrow we'll all go to Leslie and explain what happened."

Terri flashed her friends a grateful smile. Together they said good-bye to the guard, and then they headed back to the house.

AN OFF-SCRIPT SCOLDING

The next day, when the Thea Sisters JOINED their friends in the kitchen for breakfast, Matthew was there, too. Terri had asked him to come over so she could tell him what had happened the night before.

Terri looked glummer than a groundhog who's just seen his shadow. "Losing that roll of film is a **HUGE** loss for the movie . . ."

"Don't think about that now. The important thing is that you're okay," Matthew reassured her. "And it's my fault. I should have taken the film to the editing room myself . . . maybe then this WOULDN'T HAVE HAPPENED."

"My grandfather always says, 'If you always

look BACK, you never look forward,'" Violet said, sitting down at the table with a cup of tea in her paw. "That is, don't torture yourself thinking about what you should've done. Instead, think about what you can do now."

Matthew smiled at her. "You're right, Violet. The first thing to do is tell Leslie."

Terri let out a worried sigh. "She'll be madder than a cat on a mouse-free diet!"

"She'll understand," said Colette. "Come on, let's get to the studio."

But unfortunately, when they were snout-to-snout with Leslie, the director's reaction was not what they'd hoped. First she turned pale as fresh Camembert. Then her snout turned redder than a cheese rind. "Wh-what did you say?!" she sputtered at last. "LOST?! You're joking, right, Terri?

Those scenes with Johnny Ratt are irreplaceable! Ohhh, I feel dizzier than a dormouse . . ."

"I'm sorry, Leslie, I had no idea something like this would happen," Terri tried to explain. "The THIEF . . ."

"Thief?! What THIEF?!" Leslie interrupted her. "There was no thief, you silly mouse! You invented this whole story to **COVER UP** your own carelessness! Who knows where you put that film! Well, you better try to find it fast, otherwise . . ."

"**Actually**," Matthew said, stepping forward, "it's all my fault. I should have taken the

film to be stored, and —"

"Exactly!" agreed the director, waving her paw in his snout. "IT'S YOUR FAULT! BOTH OF YOUR FAULT! If you don't find that film right away, you can say good-bye to the crew, because you're fired!" With that, she turned and STOMPED AWAY.

The mouselets and Matthew looked dejected. Colette tried to rally them. "Friends, we can't let ourselves get down in the snout! The first thing we've gotta do is . . ."

"Make a plan!" Violet finished, nodding at her friend.

"Exactly! So let's review the clues," said Colette. "Um, do we have any clues?"

"Just this torn piece of paper," Paulina replied, showing the others the PAPER with the drawing of the eye she'd found on the floor in the editing room.

"Hmm, what a strange *drawing*. Does it mean anything to you, Terri?" asked Nicky.

The mouselet shook her snout.

"Okay, let's not get discouraged," Colette said. "It's possible the thief is someone from the cast or crew. Let's split up and look for CLUES. Violet, Nicky, Matthew, and I will investigate the members of the crew. Pam, Paulina, Terri, and Jenna, you . . ."

"We'll look around the studio," concluded Terri. "Come on . . .

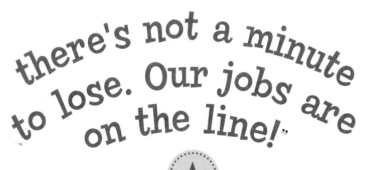

there's not a minute to lose. Our jobs are on the line!"

iNVESTiGATiONS
ON SET

While Jenna, Terri, Paulina, and Pam returned to the **EDITING** room in search of new clues, the rest of the group went to talk to the other crew members. They wanted to find out if anyone had noticed any strange rodents in the studio the night before. They didn't want the crew to panic, so they kept the missing film reel a secret for now.

First they talked to Rick, the LiGHTiNG technician, but he responded with a shake of the snout. "No, I didn't notice anything funny. I stayed a little late to check a **technical** problem. Leslie never misses a chance to remind me whenever something goes wrong. But I didn't notice anything.

Maybe you should check with Fred."

"Thanks! We'll try asking Fred," Matthew said. "He's the crew's handymouse — he works with everyone. If anything unusual happened, he'd be sure to notice it."

But Fred hadn't **noticed** anything, either. "Last night I got out of here as soon as possible. The day seemed to stretch on longer than a strand of melted mozzarella, and Leslie was in an absolutely foul mood. She argued with the sound tech, the production manager, and even with the ratlet who brings us drinks! Sorry I can't be more **helpful**."

Yesterday seemed endless!

Colette and her friends weren't ready to give up. "What if we tried asking the Powerpaw Mouselets?" asked Colette, pointing to the luxurious dressing rooms belonging to Julia, Cate, and Lindsay.

"Can't hurt to try," Matthew agreed.

Colette knocked timidly on Julia's door.

"Go away!" the actor called out.

"I . . . we . . . we just want to ask you an urgent question . . ."

"Your lies will cost you dearly!" Julia squeaked.

"But . . . but . . . I'm not lying about anything," Colette stammered.

Matthew laughed. "I don't think she's talking to you, Colette." He knocked harder. "Julia, it's Matthew. We need to squeak with you!"

A moment later, Julia opened the door with a smile.

"HI THERE! I was just going over my lines

for today's shoot. Matthew, are these your friends?"

He nodded and explained what had happened the night **before**.

But Julia hadn't seen anything, either. "I'm sorry — when I finish working I get out of here as *FAST* as the mouse who ran up the clock. I like to go take a run along the **beach**. Why don't you try asking Lindsay?"

The next Powerpaw Mouselet was nibbling on some **fruit** in her dressing room. When they told her what happened, she was really worried about Terri. "Why, that's awful! I'm so sorry to hear about it! I would have been terrified. I don't like being **closed** up in small rooms. At home in Australia, I'm

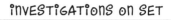
Why, that's awful!

used to wide-open spaces . . ."

"I'm Australian, too, and I also hate being shut in small SPACES," Nicky agreed.

"Really? Where are you from?" Lindsay said eagerly.

While Lindsay and Nicky chatted about Australia, Colette, Violet, and Matthew went to see the last Powerpaw Mouselet, Cate. A makeup artist was applying a thick MASK to her snout.

"Not enough here! Too much there!" Cate complained.

"She reminds me of Leslie . . ." whispered Violet, making Matthew giggle.

"What do you want?" Cate asked haughtily.

They explained everything, but Cate hadn't noticed anything, either. "Last night I went home right away. I had a terrible snoutache

from Leslie's shouting . . . that rodent is **IMPOSSIBLE!**"

"You're not the only one who thinks so," Violet observed.

Cate agreed. "With all her **screeching and shrieking**, it wouldn't surprise me if someone tried to get revenge on her."

Her WORDS struck Violet and stuck with her. Soon she was lost in thought.

"What are you thinking about?" asked Matthew, who'd caught his friend's absorbed expression.

"About what Cate said," Violet replied. "Everyone here seems to **RESENT** Leslie Mousie. Every single rodent has complained about her."

Matthew sighed. "Leslie definitely doesn't make life easy. She's a perfectionist and a bit of a drama mouse, and sometimes she **goes** overboard. But what does that have to do with what happened?"

"What if someone here stole the film reel as a PRANK?" Violet murmured.

"But who would try to sabotage a **FILM** they're working on?" Colette interjected.

Violet shrugged. "I don't know . . . It's an odd idea, but we should at least consider it."

Cate cleared her throat. She seemed **annoyed** that no one was paying attention to her. "Ahem . . . If you want to chitchat, there's plenty of room elsewhere in the studio. This spot is reserved for my beauty treatments!"

The rodents held back their giggles.

"Come on, let's find Nicky and go," Colette said.

FiNDiNG
A SUSPECT

Colette's team reunited in front of the dressing rooms. Everyone was feeling a bit **DISCOURAGED**.

"So whoever shut Terri in the storage room did it without being noticed," Nicky began.

"**Excuse me**," a small squeak interrupted.

They turned and saw Mary Lou, the makeup artist, staring at them. "I escaped for a moment," she explained, **pointing** at Cate's dressing room.

"How long do I have to stay in this mask?" Cate called.

"Another ten minutes, Cate!" Mary Lou **called** back. Then she turned back to the others. "I heard you're doing some investigating," she whispered, her eyes SHINING with excitement. "Can you tell me what it's all about?"

"Um, as we were saying, our friend was locked in a storage room and we're trying to figure out who did it," Colette said.

"But there's something else going on, right? I bet a REAL CRIME happened . . ." Mary Lou said.

The rodents exchanged a puzzled look.

"This is so exciting!" Mary Lou cried, clapping her paws. "Nothing ever happens around here."

The Thea Sisters were astounded. How could Mary Lou, who was surrounded by actors, costumes, set changes, and exciting action scenes, be . . . bored?

The makeup artist turned to Violet. "You see, I heard you say someone must resent Leslie."

"*It was just a thought . . .*" Violet said quickly.

"I never gossip, you know, but I think I know something useful," said Mary Lou. "There's one rodent who has lots of *good* reasons to be mad at Leslie: Rufus!"

Find Rufus . . .

"The production manager?" Matthew asked, surprised.

"**Yes, Him.** You know, I'm the only one who's worked with Leslie for more than a year — no one else can **put up with her**!"

Nicky giggled as Mary Lou continued. "I'm also the only one who knows that she and Rufus were engaged years ago. Then she dumped him, and he's never gotten over it."

"I don't know if that's a strong enough **Motive**," Violet said, considering.

"Wait a minute. Didn't Fred tell us that yesterday Leslie was **arguing** with the production manager?" Nicky recalled.

Mary Louuu!

"**If you ask me, he's got a grudge against her**," the makeup artist said, nodding.

"Mary Louuu! Come here!

I can't stand this MASK any longer!" Cate cried.

The makeup artist SIGHED. "Coming, coming . . ." Then she shot a look at the others. "I didn't say a word, okay?" A moment later, she'd disappeared into Cate's dressing room.

"What a peculiar rodent," Nicky commented.

"Yes," said Violet. "But she did give us a SUSPECT!"

PROFESSIONAL JEALOUSY

While Violet and the others were chatting with the makeup artist, Pam, Paulina, **Terri**, and Jenna were following up on another lead. They'd decided to investigate the sets outside the *Powerpaw Mouselets* studio. In the lot next door, a major production company was filming a movie set in ancient Egypt.

At the entrance to the studio, Pam stopped.

"What's up, Pam? Don't tell me it's **snack time** already," said Paulina, grinning.

Pam shook her snout. "Look there . . . does that remind you of anything?"

The mouselet was **pointing** to a script someone had left on a nearby table. On the first page was a *drawing* of a large eye.

"Jumping gerbil babies! It's the same as on the scrap of paper you found in the editing room," Terri cried, grabbing the script.

Paulina EXAMINED it carefully. "Not exactly — here the eye is blue. The one in the editing room was brown, with more decoration."

"I think it's the film's logo. Check this out," Terri said, pointing to a panel nearby. The set looked like a pharaoh's court, and a big reproduction of the EYE hung on the wall.

Eye on the scrap of paper

"You're right, it's definitely different." Pam sighed.

Eye on the script

"Who are you?" a grouchy squeak thundered. It belonged to a rather unfriendly-looking rodent. "Do you have PASSES?"

"Passes? We, um . . ." Paulina stammered.

"Just fans willing to do anything to SPY on the shoot, eh? And it's only the first day!" the guard shouted.

Pam was about to reply when a young rat in an elegant ancient Egyptian costume approached. "What's going on, James?"

"These rodents sneaked on set to spy on you," the GUARD explained.

"That's not true," Pam spluttered. "We're here on an INVESTIGATION!"

"Really? What kind of investigation?" the young rat asked.

Pam explained their problem to the rat, who listened carefully.

"I'm sorry, but I can't help you," he said. "We just started filming today, so I'm sure no one on the crew would know anything. Although . . ."

"YES?"

"Well, next to us is the set for *Danger Dragon*, a **SUPERHERO** film like *The Powerpaw Mouselets*. I've heard the director, John Ratantino, is very jealous of his competition."

Good luck!

"**Are you saying** he might have sabotaged Leslie's film because he was afraid it was better than his?" Jenna wondered.

"Maybe," the rat replied, shrugging.

"There you are!" a shrill squeak cried. An assistant was running their way. "Quick, get back on **set** — everyone's waiting. We can't start without you!"

"I'm coming . . ." the rat replied with a sigh.

He turned back to the Thea Sisters. "Hope that was able to help. Good luck!"

When he'd left, Terri commented, "He's just as handsome in real life as he is in the **MOVIES**, don't you think?"

"Who?" asked Paulina, perplexed.

"Don't tell me you didn't recognize him!" said Terri.

"**GREASY CAT GUTS**, who is he?" cried Pam.

"Damian Stacey — the next big thing in **HOLLYWOOD**. You know, the star of *All Thanks to the Moon*."

Paulina and Pam's WHISKERS stood on end. "That was Damian Stacey?! But he was so sweet . . ."

Terri burst out laughing. "Well, not all stars are as snooty as Johnny Ratt!"

"**Let's go** find the others and tell them

what we've learned," Jenna suggested.

Pam agreed. "Okay, but let's not say anything about Damian."

"Why not?" asked Terri.

"Because if Colette finds out we met him and didn't get his autograph, we'll be in more trouble than my uncle Bigbelly at an all-you-can-eat cheese buffet!"

The mouselets burst out laughing.

All Thanks to the Moon

Damian Stacey

A HOLE IN THE THEORY

The two groups **reunited** in front of the *Powerpaw Mouselets* studio. Each was convinced they'd found the right explanation for why the film was **stolen**.

"We realized that everyone here has, um, **SOMETHING TO SAY** about Leslie Mousie," Matthew began.

"Exactly," continued Violet. "We think we know someone who resents her enough to sabotage the movie."

"Our **suspect** is Rufus!" Nicky continued.

Terri's tail twitched. "You mean the production manager? I **work** with him sometimes."

Colette nodded. "Yes, him. Did you know

that he and Leslie were engaged once? Rumor has it he's never gotten over the breakup. And yesterday they were heard **fighting** like cats and rats."

"It all adds up," Violet said.

But Terri shook her snout. "I have to disagree — it couldn't be Rufus. Yesterday he left at six to watch his nephew's **hip-hop** performance."

Wow, amazing!

The others exchanged a look of surprise.

"He could have **COME BACK** later," Violet said.

"I don't think so," said Terri. "The performance was in Orange County, outside Los Angeles. Look, he even sent me some pictures!" Terri showed them the **text message** she'd received from Rufus.

"Looks like our theory has more holes than a slice of Swiss," Nicky said, looking down in the snout. "Did you mice learn anything?"

Jenna quickly described what they'd learned about the other **HOLLYWOOD** director making a superhero movie.

"Ratantino, of course! I heard he's been TALKING

TRASH about *The Powerpaw Mouselets,*" Matthew said.

But Violet was still lost in thought.

"What is it, Vi?" Paulina asked her.

"I just **remembered** something," she said. "This morning I was looking through the *Hollywood Star,* and I saw an article about Ratantino. CHECK IT OUT!"

HOLLYWOOD STAR
DANGER DRAGON IN DANGER OF FLOPPING?
The film is way over budget, and the production is a mess! Director John Ratantino has already left the project.

"So the **FILM** is no longer in production," said Pam.

"No more film, no more Ratantino. This says he's already **left** for San Francisco . . ."

"Then it can't be him." Jenna sighed. "We're stuck!"

CLUES!

AFTER INVESTIGATING, THE THEA SISTERS HAVE TWO POSSIBLE SUSPECTS: RUFUS AND RATANTINO. BUT BOTH HAVE GOOD ALIBIS!

WHAT IF THE THIEF DOESN'T WORK IN THE MOVIES? BUT WHO ELSE WOULD STEAL A ROLL OF FILM FROM THE SET?

An UNEXPECTED APPEARANCE

The next morning, the atmosphere at Jenna and Terri's house was gloomy. To try to lift the mood, Jenna had cooked a breakfast fit for a group of PRINCESSES.

Terri had gone to work like any other morning, but she knew Leslie would fire her if the stolen **FILM** wasn't returned very soon. So the mouselets were wracking their brains, trying to think of new leads to investigate.

Crunch! "So what can we do to help Terri?" asked Pam, chewing on a spoonful of cereal.

"I guess we should keep looking for CLUeS on set . . ." Violet sighed and munched on a pancake.

"No, mouselets," Jenna interrupted. "You've done enough. I can't let you spend your whole vacation trying to find a missing film reel."

"Oh, don't worry about us. When a friend is in trouble, the THEA SISTERS never give up!" Nicky exclaimed. "And anyway, our vacation has been fabumouse so far."

"That's true. That day on set was great!" Paulina agreed. She pulled her camera out and started looking through the pictures.

"Look: Here's Colette trying on makeup . . . Here's Violet listening to the movie score . . . And Pam STUMBLING on some cables and annoying Leslie!"

Everyone laughed. But as Paulina looked through the PHOTOS she had taken on RODEO DRIVE, Colette frowned.

Pam stumbling on set

"Wait a minute. Go back to that last photo!"

A bit confused, Paulina swiped backward.

"Zoom in on that DETAIL, please . . ."

The photo had been taken in the late afternoon, when the mouselets were leaving. There was Julia, in her green Powerpaw costume, after she'd just JUMPED onto the roof of a flaming-red sports car. Behind her were technicians and assistants.

"LOOK there . . ." said Colette.

She pointed to a figure in the

Shot on Rodeo Drive

background. It was a young rodent eating a sandwich.

Nicky squinted, focusing on the hazy figure in the picture. "**Wait**, isn't that the mouselet you noticed? The one who reminded you of someone?"

Colette smiled triumphantly. "She doesn't remind me of someone, she *is* someone. PRINCESS LANE RATLORD, to be exact!"

"What?! Are you sure?" asked Pam.

Colette nodded. "She's a mouse in a million! It's her, I'm telling you, it's Princess Lane. I'm one hundred percent certain!"

"Well, she doesn't look so ROYAL. She's really scarfing down that sandwich!" Paulina said.

"But what is she doing here in Los Angeles?" asked Jenna.

"I have no idea," Colette replied.

"Sisters, this is incredible! We were looking for a film thief, and instead we found a RUNAWAY princess!" said Pam.

The other mouselets all laughed.

"Do you know what I think? You should solve this MYSTERY," said Jenna. "Isn't that your thing?"

"But what about your sister?" asked Violet.

"She'll get through it. I'm sure we'll figure something out. Besides, Lane's case is of international importance," Jenna replied.

"Are you saying we should alert the police?" asked Violet.

"NO WAY!" cried Colette. "If Lane is here, she must have a reason. We should find her and make sure she's okay."

"Great idea," said Pam. "But how?"

For a few moments, the room was silent. The only sound was Pam chewing (she hadn't finished her breakfast yet).

"Well," began Violet, "let's make an educated guess. Where would you go if you were a princess and found yourself in Los Angeles?"

"But we're not squeaking about just any

princess — it's Lane Ratlord! She's sunny, sporty, and spontaneous," Colette protested.

Violet smiled. "Perfect. That's exactly the kind of place where we should look for her:

somewhere sunny, sporty, and spontaneous!"

FLYING — ON
SKATES!

Colette pulled out her pink notepad and began to make a list of everything she knew about Princess Lane.

LANE LIKES:

1. VANILLA ICE CREAM
2. SKATING
3. MOVIES
4. SPORTS
5. ROCK MUSIC

The mouselets hoped the list would give them ideas of places to start their search.

"If she **loves** the movies, that explains why she was so interested in the **FILM** shoot," Violet reflected.

"And if one of her passions is skating, she might be hanging out in Venice," Jenna observed.

"Yes! I want to visit Venice, too!" cried Nicky, clapping.

Paulina looked confused. "Wait, you mean Venice, the city in **ITALY**?"

"Come on, Paulina, didn't you read the guidebook?" Nicky teased. "Venice is also a neighborhood in LA. It got its name because it's built with **canals**, just like the original Venice."

"**IT'S TRUE**," Jenna confirmed. "Now it's famouse for its boardwalk along the beach.

Plus it has bike paths that are perfect for rodents who like to *skate*."

"All right, you've convinced me. Let's make like a cheese wheel and roll!" Paulina said.

An hour later, the THEA SISTERS were admiring the turquoise-blue ocean that stretches past the palm trees of Venice Beach.

"Pam, BE CAREFUL!" shouted Paulina.

Pam barely had time to duck out of the way as a ratlet did a DARING flip on his unicycle, and then sped past her.

"It'd be better if we got some wheels, don't you think?" said Pam.

"We can rent skates over there," said Jenna, pointing to a store nearby.

While Pam strapped on the in-line skates Jenna had sent her, the others rented them.

They snapped on their helmets and

kneepads and started to make their way across the **length** and **breadth** of the magnificent boardwalk that borders the sea.

"Look over there," Colette said, gazing at the painted walls that looked like true **WORKS OF ART**.

"And over there!" cried Nicky, pointing to a group of acrobats.

"Venice Beach is **FAMOUS** for its street artists," Jenna explained.

"It's definitely a cool place to visit. But unfortunately there's no **SIGN** of the princess here . . ." Violet said sadly.

FOUL ON THE PLAY

Together, the little group headed for a spot where a popular **R⚬CK BanD** would be playing, but all they could do was look around helplessly, because they didn't have tickets.

"I'm starting to think this wasn't such a *brilliant* way to find Lane," Violet reflected.

"Come on, Vi, don't lose hope! We've got one more lead to follow: Lane loves SPORTS! Jenna, do you know if there are any big games happening around here?"

"There's probably a FOOTBALL GAME, but I'm not sure," Jenna replied. "Let me call

Matthew and ask him. He's a huge football fan."

The ratlet confirmed there was an important game that **EVENiNG**. The six friends made plans to meet him later at the stadium.

Then Jenna called Terri to make sure she was okay. Her sister said it had been a rough day at the studio, so she wanted to stay home to rest.

"This is my first time at a FOOTBALL game," Colette commented as they scurried into the stadium. "I've seen games on TV, but I've never actually gone to one."

"I love going to games!" said Pam, looking around. Lots of fans were dressed in the home team's jerseys. Some had even PAiNTED their snouts the team colors!

Colette beamed. "It's like everyone is in

costume for the game!"

Matthew laughed. "You've really got Hollywood on the brain, Colette!"

"I don't know much about football," said Violet. "Is there a lot of **Strategy** involved?"

Matthew nodded. "There sure is. You need strategies to hide your defensive plans, to figure out the other team's tactics, and to plan your moves!"

Violet's eyes widened. "Really? It sounds like CHESS. I love chess!"

"I thought so," Matthew said, winking. "You'll like football, you'll see!"

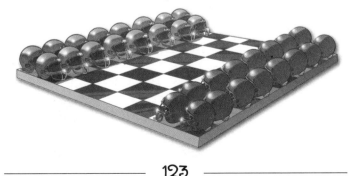

"Definitely!" said Paulina. "This is going to more **FUN** than a trip to CheeseFest."

The rodents found their seats. Matthew started to comment on the **action** while the mouselets scanned the crowd for signs of the princess.

After the kickoff, Jenna and the other Thea Sisters got caught up in the game, too. The **STADIUM** was alive with cheers from the fans, who waved banners and shouted chants to root their TEAM on.

When the home TEAM scored a touchdown, the Thea Sisters JUMPED to their paws to celebrate with the crowd.

"Did you see that play?" Pam said. She **loved** football.

"Uh-huh," said Paulina. "You saw it, right, Coco?"

Colette wasn't paying attention to what Paulina was saying. She was staring into the crowd.

"It's **HER**!" she cried, pointing to a mouselet about fifteen feet away. She was wearing **sunglasses** and a baseball cap. When she jumped up to celebrate, a few blonde curls had escaped from the cap.

"Are you sure?" asked Jenna.

Colette was already scampering through the crowd to try and reach the princess. The others quickly followed.

Unfortunately, it wasn't easy to get through the **MOB** of fans. They were waiting in lines for snacks and souvenirs, and everyone was moving in **different** directions. Finally, when the mouselets and Matthew were just a few feet away from Lane, she **noticed** them.

The princess **turned away** and started to run, slipping through the crowd. But Nicky, who was the most **ATHLETIC** of the group, managed to stay right on her tail.

Please, wait for me! Don't run away!

FiNALLY . . .
CAUGHT!

Weaving through flocks of fans, Colette, Pam, Paulina, Violet, Jenna, and Matthew hurried after Nicky and Lane toward the STaDiUM exit.

"Please, stop!" Nicky called. She reached out and finally managed to **grab** Lane's paw.

The others soon joined them and circled around the PRINCESS, who looked upset.

"Who are you? Why are you following me? I'm not going home, all right?!"

"It's okay, Lane," said Colette. "We're not here to take you home."

"Then **what** do you want?" asked Lane. During the chase, her cap had slipped off, and her famous golden locks fluttered over her shoulders. Her sunglasses slid down her snout, revealing bright emerald EYES.

"We just want to find out why you *RAN AWAY*," Colette said kindly. "Don't you know your family is very worried about you? Your disappearance is all over the news!"

Lane sighed. "I know, and I'm sorry. I wasn't trying to make them worry."

"Then why did you leave?" Paulina asked.

"I just wanted to be **FREE**," Lane explained.

"What do you mean?" asked Violet.

"I know my life seems absolutely marvemouse," Lane said. "And I am very lucky. I can have all the clothes I **want**, I get to go on vacation in all the most exclusive places, I've got maids and butlers

I always have to:

Dress in fancy clothes . . .

Stay with my bodyguard . . .

It's so boring!

waiting on me. But that's not what I want!"

"So what do you want?" asked Nicky.

Lane looked into the **MOUSELETS'** eyes. It was as if she was trying to figure out if she could trust them. "Just to be a regular, ordinary mouselet like you," she said at last. "Not to always have someone watching me, making sure I follow the rules. I never get to do anything — I always have to remember that I'm the heir to the THRONE of Mousitania . . ."

"That doesn't sound too bad to me," Matthew replied.

"**YOU DON'T UNDERSTAND!**" Lane cried. "Everything I want to do isn't proper for a princess! **I CAN'T** go to the movies, go skating, or even eat a sandwich on the street . . ."

"All the things that you've done here in Los Angeles, right?" asked Colette, who was beginning to understand.

Lane nodded. "I wanted to be totally **FREE** for once in my life. I came here because this is the

Here, I can:

Go skating!

Go to the movies!

Eat a sandwich on the street!

movie capital of the world. This is the place my **dreams** can come true! Is that too much to ask?"

The princess's squeak was trembling, and her eyes shone with tears.

The mouselets gazed at her sympathetically. Then Pam started to GIGGLE.

All a princess wants is . . . a good sandwich!

"Pam, what is it?" asked Paulina, surprised.

"I was just thinking about the fact that so many mouselets wish they were princesses, with all the clothes, jewelry, and fabumouse parties. Then we meet a real princess and discover that all she wants is to be a regular mouselet — to go skating and eat junk food whenever she feels like it!"

Everyone laughed, even Lane. Pam had broken the TENSION.

"Let's get out of here," Jenna suggested. "Lane, if you want to spend an evening like a normal mouselet, come on over for dinner. You've probably had enough of being alone and in disguise, right?"

A smile spread across the princess's famouse snout. "Yes, thank you!"

As they headed away from the stadium, Pam let out a big SIGH. "I was really looking forward to seeing the rest of the game!"

"Be *patient*, Pam, we'll have another chance sooner or later," Violet laughed.

But just then she felt a chill run down her tail. Someone was watching her and her friends, she was sure of it! Was there someone besides the Thea Sisters following Lane?

CLUES!
IS SOMEONE FOLLOWING LANE AND THE THEA SISTERS? WHO COULD IT BE? AND WHY?

A STRANGER
IN THE SHADOWS

Violet turned around and checked the parking lot, which was filled with **shadows**. There didn't seem to be anyone there. But Violet still had the sensation of being watched.

SUDDENLY, she heard a tiny scrape to her left. She turned to check a dark corner of the parking lot. Who was there?

"Hey, I think someone's over there," Violet told her **friends**.

The others turned in that **direction**. They spotted a rodent who looked like a security guard, with a cap pulled low on his head.

"Look at the symbol on his jacket!" Colette whispered.

"It's the same EYE that's on the piece of paper from the editing room!" Nicky said.

The rodent realized he was being observed, and quickly turned away.

"Hey, excuse me!" Matthew called, taking a few steps toward him.

But the rodent began running in the opposite direction.

"LET'S FOLLOW HIM!" cried Jenna. "Maybe he knows something about the missing film reel!"

This time it was Pam who led the CHASE. In a few strides, she'd crossed the lot and almost reached the mysterious rodent, who squeezed between one car and the next. Just when Pam was about to catch him, the rodent

SWERVED toward the parking lot exit. But he didn't fool Pam! She lunged forward and threw herself against the mouse, **TRIPPING HIM**.

The others raced over to the pair, who were sprawled on the ground.

"**Great tackle, Pam!** You're ready to play football like a pro," Nicky couldn't help joking. She extended a  to help her friend up.

The unknown rodent also got to his paws,

Not so fast!

looking worse than a hamster who'd just fallen off his wheel.

"**WHO** are you? **WHY** did you run? And **WHAT** does this logo mean?" asked Violet all in one breath, pointing to the **EYE** printed on his clothes.

"I think I should get out of here," Lane murmured, stuffing her cap back on her head so he wouldn't recognize her.

"No, wait, don't go," the rodent said. "Let me explain everything to you, and to you, too, PRINCESS . . ."

Lane **JUMPED**. "You recognize me?"

"Of course, Your Highness, I know very well who you are. In fact, *I know who all of you are!*"

A DOUBLE
SURPRISE

The friends were stunned. None of them had ever seen this rodent before!

"MOLDY MOZZARELLA! You better start squeaking fast, because we don't have a clue who you are," Pam declared.

The rodent cleared his throat. "My name is Elliott, and I am a private investigator from Mousitania."

The princess was startled. "But then . . ."

The rodent nodded. "Yes, Princess Lane, after you disappeared, the royal family asked me to keep track of you."

"I knew it!" shouted Lane, STAMPING her paw. "I bet you couldn't wait to find me, take me home, and collect your reward!"

Elliott **smiled**. "I didn't find you this evening. I've been following you for several days."

"But . . . but why?" asked the princess, **astounded**. "Were you going to let me stay here instead of completing your mission?"

I've been following you for several days!

But why?

"**No, not at all**," replied the rodent. "My mission was to find you and watch over you as long as you stayed in Los Angeles. Your parents simply want to make sure you are safe."

Lane was more confused than a cat in a dog kennel. "Are you saying that my parents know I'm on *vacation* like a normal mouselet . . . and they're okay with it?"

Elliott **nodded**. "They love you very much, and they know that a mouselet your age needs to feel **FREE**. They only asked that I protect the PRINCESS and her image."

"What do you mean?" Pam asked.

I will look out for Princess Lane!

"It's what I was trying to tell you earlier, mouselets," Lane **explained**. "When you're part of the royal family, the public is always watching you. No one must see a princess doing anything embarrassing, like **yawning** at a press conference, or spilling on a dress, or . . ."

"Or following a big star around Hollywood!" cried Colette, thinking of the PHOTO that showed Lane on the SET of *The Powerpaw Mouselets.*

"Now I get it!" cried Violet.

Everyone turned to look at her. "For a princess, it's a problem if you follow a movie crew around . . . and an even bigger problem if you're caught on **film**!"

"What? I still don't get it," said Colette.

"Leslie's crew ended up Filming Lane the day they were shooting in the city, right, Elliott?" said Violet.

The investigator nodded. "Exactly. Now do you understand why I had to take the film? I couldn't RISK the whole world seeing the runaway princess. We have to protect her privacy. If anyone realized that was her in the movie, it'd be a huge story, and all the news reporters in the world would be trailing her around, asking why she'd run away."

Pam smacked herself in the snout. "Now I get it! So the eye on your cap and on the scrap of paper is just your company logo. *You* are the MYSTERIOUS thief!"

Elliott sighed sheepishly. "Um . . . yes. I'm very sorry about that."

"So it's just **coincidence** that the shoot next door had a similar logo," said Paulina.

"Yes," said Elliott, nodding. "And I'm sorry I needed to trick your friend and lock her up . . . I hope she wasn't too scared!"

Jenna was OUTRAGED. "How could you treat my sister that way?"

"I'm truly very **sorry**. I didn't know what else to do," Elliott replied. "I hope I'll be able to apologize in person."

"You can do that when you return the film to the crew," Matthew said STERNLY.

Elliott pulled his whiskers. "But I can't return it! There are scenes showing the princess!"

"Don't worry. **I know just what to do**," Matthew assured him.

THE CUT OF AN ARTIST!

The next day at dawn, eight **FIGURES** scampered into the studio. They quickly passed through **ROOMS** full of cables and spotlights and slipped through the door of the editing room.

"Watch out for that table . . ." warned a male squeak.

"**OWWWWW!**" cried a nearby mouse.

"Pam, are you okay?"

"Yes," she replied. "Sorry, Matthew."

"Remember, we must be quiet as mice," Violet said. "No one can know we're here."

"It's okay, Violet," Terri said. "The studio is deserted right now. Shooting won't start for another hour."

"Come on — we've got things to do," said Matthew. "Nicky, do you have the film?"

Nicky **rummaged** through her purse for a minute, and then pulled out a film reel and pawed it to her friend.

"Are you sure you can do this?" asked Violet.

The ratlet nodded. "**OF COURSE!** As I explained to Elliott, I only need to cut the scenes that show Lane. We just have to find them all."

The day before, the rodents had convinced the INVESTIGATOR from Mousitania to paw over the stolen film. They'd promised to delete all the scenes in which PRINCESS LANE appeared. And the only one who could do a job like that was Matthew, since he'd mastered the software for editing film.

The ratlet began to view each scene and, **TAKE** after **TAKE**, delete all the

Almost there!

incriminating frames. After a half hour of work, he cried, "Done!"

Just then, Paulina RAN in. She'd been keeping watch outside.

"A car's coming," she announced, worried. "How close are you?"

"We're done," Terri assured her. She peeked outside. "Hey, that's Leslie's car. She's here early," she said in surprise.

The rodents left the EDITING room just as the director scurried into the studio.

Terri and Matthew took a deep breath and scampered right up to Leslie Mousie.

"YOU?! You're still here?" the director spluttered. "I told you I didn't want to see you on this set!"

"Actually, we're here to give you this," said Terri.

Leslie raised an eyebrow, skeptical. But

when she opened the package, her harsh expression MELTED, and a smile spread across her snout. "This is . . ."

"Yes," Matthew said. "We found the missing film."

"But how . . . ? Where . . . ?" Leslie asked, confused but pleased.

"Well . . . it's a long story," Terri said. "But we've got a movie to shoot, right?"

The director narrowed her eyes and looked at the group of rodents. Then she grinned. "I have a feeling you rodents have quite a tale for the telling . . ."

Jenna LOOKED at her friends and winked. "Our story is an awful lot like the

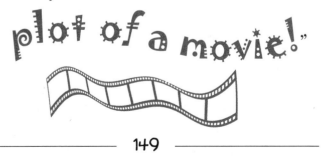

plot of a movie!"

LiKE A nORmAL MOUSELET

The **THEA SiSTERS** said good-bye to Terri, Jenna, and Matthew and scurried back to **DOWNTOWN** Los Angeles. They had one last mission: to say good-bye to their new friend Lane before she headed home to Mousitania.

The day before, the princess had made **plans** to meet the Thea Sisters in her hotel lobby for a last farewell. But when the mouselets arrived, there was no **TRACE** of her.

"Maybe she already left," said Colette. "She had a flight in the early afternoon . . ."

"**OH NO**," Violet moaned. "We shouldn't have stopped to get that slice of pizza, Pam.

It made us late . . ."

"No, it was a great idea!" cried a happy squeak behind them.

"Lane! You haven't left yet!" Colette said with a sigh of relief. Then, looking closer, she added, "But . . . why don't you have any LUGGAGE?"

The princess was smiling wider than a triple-cheese sandwich. "Mouselets, I have marvemouse news. My parents said I could stay for another day, so . . ."

"So let's not waste any time!" Nicky declared. "I've got the perfect plan. I know where we can spend a super afternoon!"

A moment later, the mouselets were in a taxi zooming toward the coast. It dropped them off in front of a large pier, where a tall ferris wheel towered over them.

"Welcome to Santa Monica!" Nicky announced. "We can visit the aquarium, take a walk on the beach, ride on the merry-go-round . . ."

"And get a banana split with melted cheese on top!" Pam finished.

The mouselets grinned and plunged into the pier's whirl of colors and sounds. Here Lane could finally spend a day of fun like a normal mouselet. She even agreed to a ride on the Ferris wheel.

When the TIME finally came to say good-bye, a sad look passed over Lane's snout. The mouselets immediately understood what their new friend was thinking, and they squeezed around her.

"Lane," said Colette, "your parents were very kind to give you an extra day, but the whole world has been holding its breath waiting for you."

"I know — it's time to go back. It's just that . . . I wish that this trip weren't over," Lane replied. "As soon as I get back home, I'll go back to my old life, and I'll be so lonely!"

The THEA SiSTERS noticed a tear making tracks down her cheek.

"You're wrong. You won't be alone. You have us now! And true friends are forever," Colette said.

The Thea Sisters wrapped their paws around the princess in a **great big hug**. Lane grinned and returned their embrace.

PREMIERE OF A MOUSTERPIECE!

Six months later, the Thea Sisters were back in **HOLLYWOOD**. Leslie Mousie had invited them to the world premiere of *The Powerpaw Mouselets*!

Jenna picked them up at the airport, and they all hurried back to her house to change. They had just slipped into their most elegant clothes when a horn honked out in the street.

"That's our limousine! Leslie sent it. She's so happy about the *film's premiere* that she's throwing around money like grated mozzarella!" Jenna said, winking.

"Wow, I feel like a real star," Pam said as they scrambled in.

A half hour later, they reached the movie theater. As they hopped out of the limo, Violet started to scan the crowd.

"I think I know who you're looking for, Vi . . ." Colette teased.

"What are you talking about? I'm not looking for anyone!" her friend replied, **blushing** to the roots of her fur. "Just

What a dream!

looking for CELEBRITIES."

"Oh, really?" Colette said SLYLY. "Then you probably don't care that Matthew's right over there . . ."

"Where?" Violet immediately replied. Then she saw him. The young assistant director was dressed in an elegant tuxedo.

"I'm so happy to see you again, Violet," Matthew said. "I hope you LIKE the final cut!"

He led her toward one of the front rows. But someone blocked their way, shouting, "IT CAN'T BE! IT'S A TRAGEDY! IT'S A CAT-ASTROPHE!"

"Leslie, what happened?" asked Terri.

"Is there a problem with the projector?" Matthew asked.

"No! I just BROKE a heel!"

Everyone burst out laughing. After a

moment of surprise, Leslie joined in. "Maybe I was **exaggerating** about the cat-astrophe . . ." she admitted.

"Just keep calm and scurry on," Terri declared.

They all sat down together. The theater was **PACKED** — everywhere the mouselets looked, there were movie fans, actors, and directors.

Two hours later, the words **THE END** appeared on the screen. The three heroines scurried onstage. Thunderous applause greeted them. Then it was Leslie's turn to take a bow.

From the **FRONT ROW**, the Thea Sisters looked on, beaming.

They had found new friends, solved a mystery, and saved a movie mousterpiece!

Don't miss any Thea Sisters adventures!

Thea Stilton and the Dragon's Code

Thea Stilton and the Mountain of Fire

Thea Stilton and the Ghost of the Shipwreck

Thea Stilton and the Secret City

Thea Stilton and the Mystery in Paris

Thea Stilton and the Cherry Blossom Adventure

Thea Stilton and the Star Castaways

Thea Stilton: Big Trouble in the Big Apple

Thea Stilton and the Ice Treasure

Thea Stilton and the Secret of the Old Castle

Thea Stilton and the Blue Scarab Hunt

Thea Stilton and the Prince's Emerald

Thea Stilton and the Mystery on the Orient Express

Thea Stilton and the Dancing Shadows

Thea Stilton and the Legend of the Fire Flowers

Thea Stilton and the Spanish Dance Mission

Thea Stilton and the Journey to the Lion's Den

Thea Stilton and the Great Tulip Heist

Thea Stilton and the Chocolate Sabotage

Thea Stilton and the Missing Myth

Thea Stilton and the Lost Letters

Thea Stilton and the Tropical Treasure

Thea Stilton and the Hollywood Hoax

Up Next!

Thea Stilton and the Madagascar Madness

Check out my fabumouse special editions!

THE JOURNEY TO ATLANTIS

THE SECRET OF THE FAIRIES

THE SECRET OF THE SNOW

THE CLOUD CASTLE

THE TREASURE OF THE SEA

Be sure to read all my fabumouse adventures!

#1 Lost Treasure of the Emerald Eye

#2 The Curse of the Cheese Pyramid

#3 Cat and Mouse in a Haunted House

#4 I'm Too Fond of My Fur!

#5 Four Mice Deep in the Jungle

#6 Paws Off, Cheddarface!

#7 Red Pizzas for a Blue Count

#8 Attack of the Bandit Cats

#9 A Fabumouse Vacation for Geronimo

#10 All Because of a Cup of Coffee

#11 It's Halloween, You 'Fraidy Mouse!

#12 Merry Christmas, Geronimo!

#13 The Phantom of the Subway

#14 The Temple of the Ruby of Fire

#15 The Mona Mousa Code

#16 A Cheese-Colored Camper

#17 Watch Your Whiskers, Stilton!

#18 Shipwreck on the Pirate Islands

#19 My Name Is Stilton, Geronimo Stilton

#20 Surf's Up, Geronimo!

#21 The Wild, Wild West

#22 The Secret of Cacklefur Castle

A Christmas Tale

#23 Valentine's Day Disaster

#24 Field Trip to Niagara Falls

#25 The Search for Sunken Treasure

#26 The Mummy with No Name

#27 The Christmas Toy Factory

#28 Wedding Crasher

#29 Down and Out Down Under

#30 The Mouse Island Marathon

#31 The Mysterious Cheese Thief

Christmas Catastrophe

#32 Valley of the Giant Skeletons

#33 Geronimo and the Gold Medal Mystery

#34 Geronimo Stilton, Secret Agent

#35 A Very Merry Christmas

#36 Geronimo's Valentine

#37 The Race Across America

#38 A Fabumouse School Adventure

#39 Singing Sensation

#40 The Karate Mouse

#41 Mighty Mount Kilimanjaro

#42 The Peculiar Pumpkin Thief

#43 I'm Not a Supermouse!

#44 The Giant Diamond Robbery

#45 Save the White Whale!

#46 The Haunted Castle

#47 Run for the Hills, Geronimo!

#48 The Mystery in Venice

#49 The Way of the Samurai

#50 This Hotel Is Haunted!

#51 The Enormouse Pearl Heist

#52 Mouse in Space!

#53 Rumble in the Jungle

#54 Get into Gear, Stilton!

#55 The Golden Statue Plot

#56 Flight of the Red Bandit

The Hunt for the Golden Book

#57 The Stinky Cheese Vacation

#58 The Super Chef Contest

#59 Welcome to Moldy Manor

The Hunt for the Curious Cheese

#60 The Treasure of Easter Island

#61 Mouse House Hunter

#62 Mouse Overboard!

The Hunt for the Secret Papyrus

#63 The Cheese Experiment

#64 Magical Mission

Meet
GERONIMO STILTONOOT

He is a cavemouse — Geronimo Stilton's ancient ancestor! He runs the stone newspaper in the prehistoric village of Old Mouse City. From dealing with dinosaurs to dodging meteorites, his life in the Stone Age is full of adventure!

#1 The Stone of Fire

#2 Watch Your Tail!

#3 Help, I'm in Hot Lava!

#4 The Fast and the Frozen

#5 The Great Mouse Race

#6 Don't Wake the Dinosaur!

#7 I'm a Scaredy-Mouse!

#8 Surfing for Secrets

#9 Get the Scoop, Geronimo!

#10 My Autosaurus Will Win!

#11 Sea Monster Surprise

#12 Paws Off the Pearl!

MEET
GERONIMO STILTONIX

He is a spacemouse — the Geronimo Stilton of a parallel universe! He is captain of the spaceship *MouseStar 1*. While flying through the cosmos, he visits distant planets and meets crazy aliens. His adventures are out of this world!

#1 Alien Escape

#2 You're Mine, Captain!

#3 Ice Planet Adventure

#4 The Galactic Goal

#5 Rescue Rebellion

#6 The Underwater Planet

#7 Beware! Space Junk!

#8 Away in a Star Sled

Meet
CREEPELLA VON CACKLEFUR

Geronimo Stilton, have a lot of mouse friends, but none as **spooky** as my friend CREEPELLA VON CACKLEFUR! She is an enchanting and MYSTERIOUS mouse with a pet bat named **Bitewing.** YIKES! I'm a real 'fraidy mouse, but even I think CREEPELLA and her family are AWFULLY fascinating. I can't wait for you to read all about CREEPELLA in these a-mouse-ly funny and **spectacularly spooky** tales!

#1 The Thirteen Ghosts

#2 Meet Me in Horrorwood

#3 Ghost Pirate Treasure

#4 Return of the Vampire

#5 Fright Night

#6 Ride for Your Life!

#7 A Suitcase Full of Ghosts

#8 The Phantom of the Theater

THANKS FOR READING, AND GOOD-BYE UNTIL OUR NEXT ADVENTURE!